For Elisa Johnston,
who loves learning, rivers, and seas
—Deborah Hopkinson

To LaVonne,
my bride of 44 years
—Ron Husband

For information address Disney • Hyperion, 125 West End Avenue, New York, New York 10023.
Printed in Malaysia
First Edition, June 2016
1 3 5 7 9 10 8 6 4 2
FAC-029191-16046

Library of Congress Cataloging-in-Publication Data

Hopkinson, Deborah.
Steamboat school / written by Deborah Hopkinson ; illustrated by Ron Husband.
pages cm
"Inspired by a true story."
"St. Louis, Missouri: 1847."
Summary: In 1847 St. Louis, Missouri, when a new law against educating African Americans forces Reverend John to close his school, he finds an ingenious solution to the new state law by moving his school to a steamboat in the Mississippi River. Includes author's note on Reverend John Berry Meachum, a minister, entrepreneur, and educator who fought tirelessly for the rights of African Americans.
Includes bibliographical references.
ISBN 978-1-4231-2196-1—ISBN 1-4231-2196-1
1. Meachum, John B., 1789—-Juvenile fiction. [1. Meachum, John B., 1789—-Fiction. 2. Education—Fiction. 3. African Americans—Fiction.] I. Husband, Ron, illustrator. II. Title.
PZ7.H778125Su 2016
[E]—dc23 2015016315

Reinforced binding
Visit www.DisneyBooks.com

STEAMBOAT SCHOOL

Inspired by a True Story

ST. LOUIS, MISSOURI: 1847

by Deborah Hopkinson Illustrated by Ron Husband

DISNEY • HYPERION
LOS ANGELES NEW YORK

I always thought being brave
was for grown-up heroes doing big, daring deeds.
But Mama says that sometimes courage
is just an ordinary boy like me
doing a small thing, as small as picking up a pencil.

THE CANDLE SCHOOL

I might as well begin with that first morning,
when Mama made such a fuss over my going to school.
"Ouch! My face isn't a washboard," I cried.
She kept scrubbing.

"James, this is a proud day,"
she said.

Truth was, Tassie had to drag me all the way.
I wanted to stop and see everything:
the steamboats dotting the river, their black smokestacks straight as pencils;
the levee bustling with men loading and unloading—
sugarcane, cotton, wheat, and logs for the sawmills.
River bells clanged.
People shouted and scurried like ants.

"Hurry," urged Tassie. "Reverend John doesn't hold with being late."
At Third and Almond, we slipped into the church,
and headed down the basement steps,
into the darkness,
to the Tallow Candle School.

"Why can't we have windows?" I whined, already missing the sun.
"Hush, you know why," Tassie said.
And I did.

I felt a hand on my shoulder.
"Welcome to school, James," said Reverend John.

"We make our own light here."

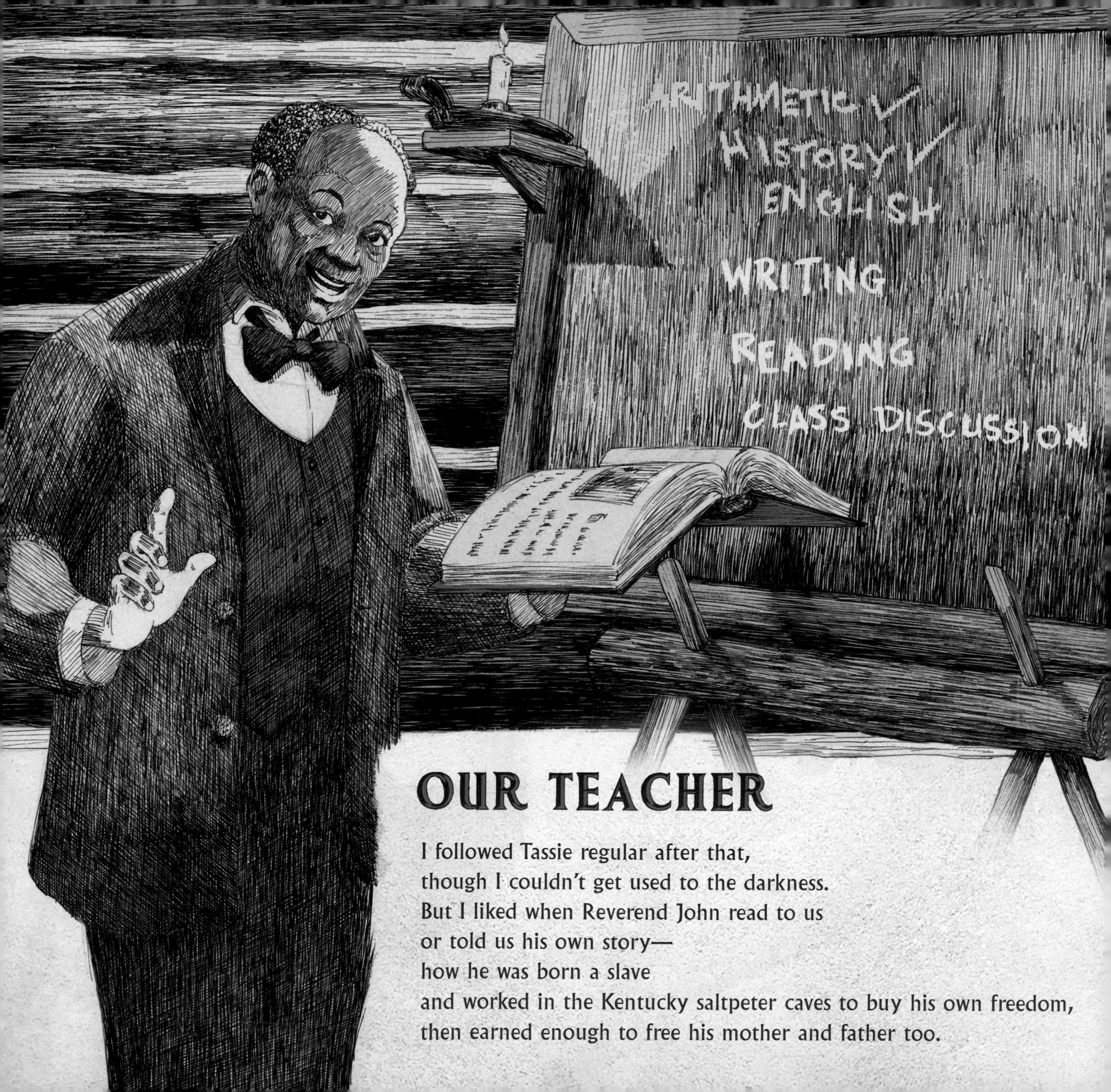

OUR TEACHER

I followed Tassie regular after that,
though I couldn't get used to the darkness.
But I liked when Reverend John read to us
or told us his own story—
how he was born a slave
and worked in the Kentucky saltpeter caves to buy his own freedom,
then earned enough to free his mother and father too.

But before he could buy liberty for his wife,
her master brought her here to St. Louis.
Reverend John followed, walking hundreds of miles.
"I arrived with three dollars," he told us.
"But you had to pay two dollars to cross the Mississippi!" we chimed in.
He laughed and held out his hands.

"All I needed was that one dollar and my two hands, to start again."

Reverend John went to work as a barrel maker and carpenter.
He earned enough to free his wife. Then, he became
the first leader of this church.
He believed in hard work and learning.
He believed in us too.

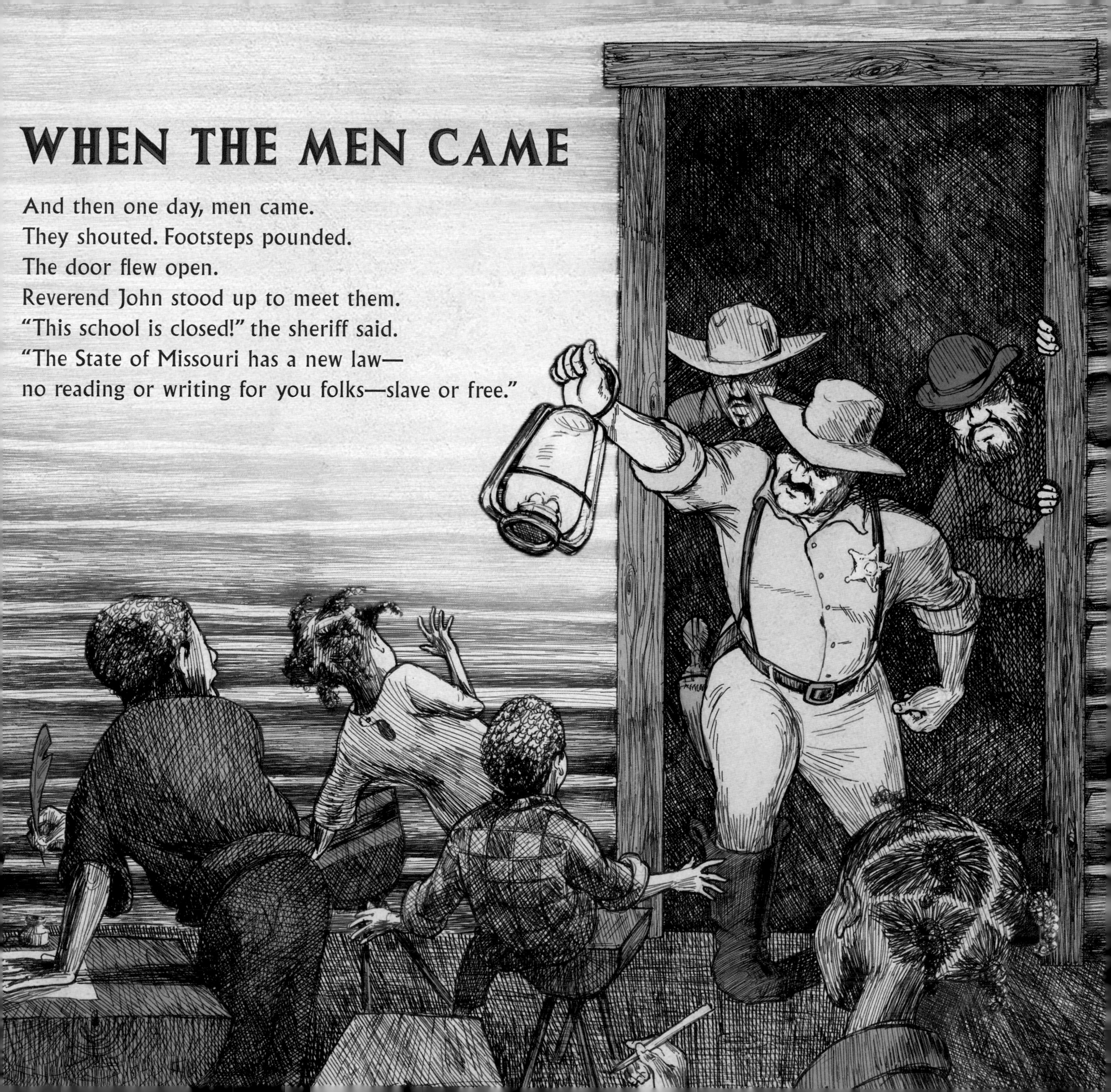

WHEN THE MEN CAME

And then one day, men came.
They shouted. Footsteps pounded.
The door flew open.
Reverend John stood up to meet them.
"This school is closed!" the sheriff said.
"The State of Missouri has a new law—
no reading or writing for you folks—slave or free."

THE NEW LAW: 1847

Later, I asked Reverend John to write out the law on a scrap of paper.

"Be it enacted by the General Assembly of the State of Missouri, as follows:

No person shall keep any school for the instruction of negroes or mulattoes, reading or writing, in this State."

FINDING A WAY

That night Tassie's tears glistened on her cheeks,
as shiny as her needle in the lamplight.
"What will happen now?" she asked.

I thought of all those days Tassie had dragged me to school.
Now I felt as if a penny I'd counted on
had fallen out of my pocket.

"Reverend John Berry Meachum cares more for education than any man in this city," Mama said.

"He's a force like the Mississippi River itself. And like the river, he'll find a way."

I didn't see how, though.
I took out my scrap of paper and read the law again.

We waited, but no word came.
At night I made letters and numbers by candlelight.

By day I toted bundles of laundry for Mama and practiced reading signs:

Dry Goods. Horses to Let. Stable. Barber. Potatoes. I closed my eyes. *Horses.*

"H-O-R-S-E-S."

One morning my steps took me to the church.
I thought of our books and slates in that dark room.
Funny how something you don't care much about at first
can end up becoming the most important part of you.

The door opened and Reverend John stepped out.
"Hello, James. If you're done helping your mother today, come along with me."
He led the way to the levee, to a bright new steamboat.
"She's a real beauty," I said. "Did you build her, sir?"
For answer he held up his two hands.
"I could use some help now, though," he said.

Tassie and I helped every day after that:
painting, hammering, and polishing the deck.
"What's inside?" I asked one day.
"Hush," said Tassie. "Don't you know?"
And I did.

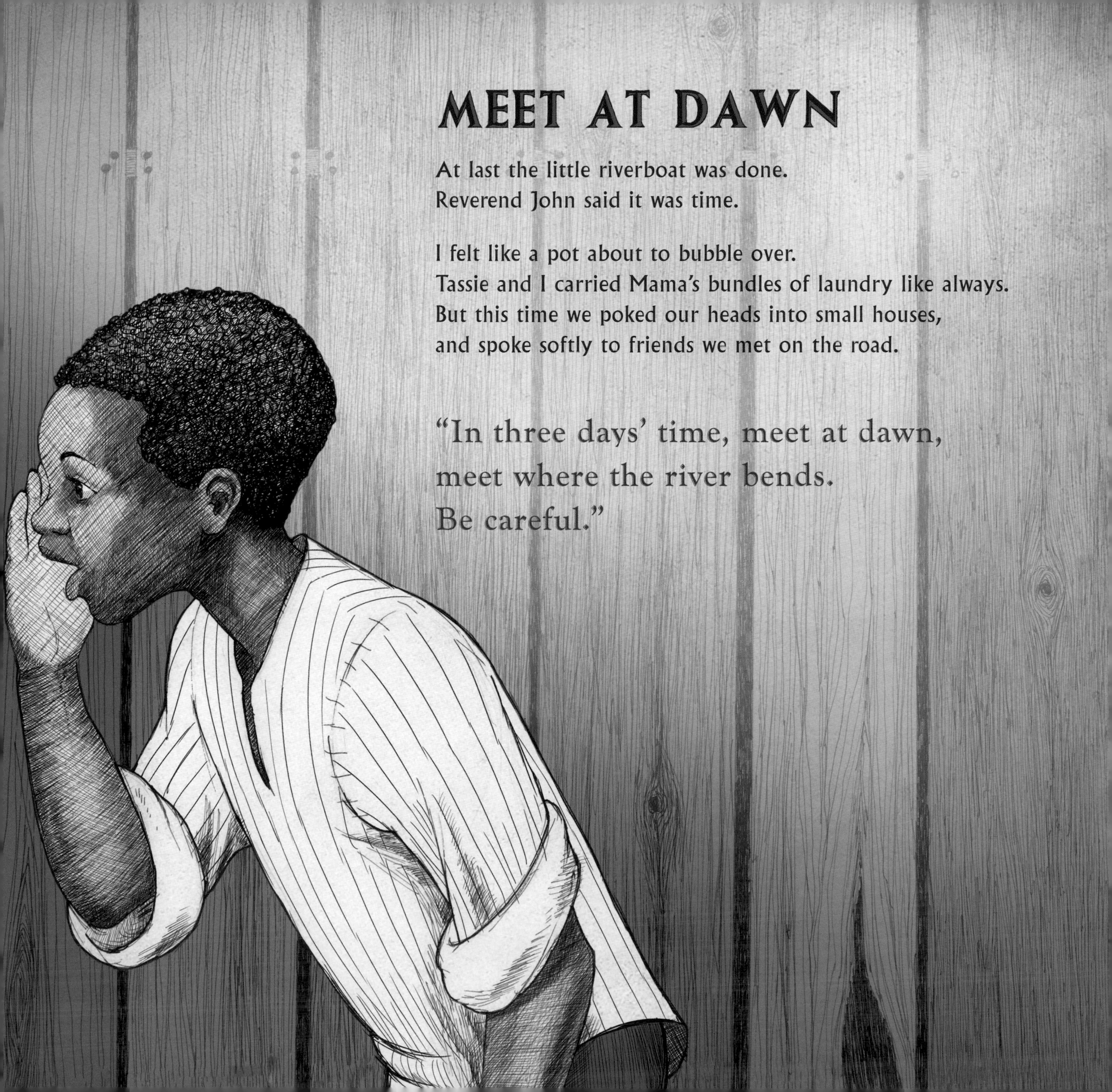

MEET AT DAWN

At last the little riverboat was done.
Reverend John said it was time.

I felt like a pot about to bubble over.
Tassie and I carried Mama's bundles of laundry like always.
But this time we poked our heads into small houses,
and spoke softly to friends we met on the road.

"In three days' time, meet at dawn,
meet where the river bends.
Be careful."

DIPPING THE OAR

The streets were dark when Tassie and I set out.
We walked quickly by the levee.
Suddenly I turned a corner and bumped into a policeman.
"Where are you two going?" he growled.
"We're freedmen, sir. Our mother's a laundress," I squeaked out.
Tassie nodded. "We're fetching two big bundles of laundry for her."
He grunted, and waved us on.
We ran the rest of the way.

In the gray fog, the river smelled like mud.
I pointed. "There! He's over there."
We climbed into the skiff.
Our teacher dipped his oar into the still, deep water.

"But I don't see anything," someone whispered.
Then a breeze lifted the fog a little,
and we saw a boat anchored in the river.
"That's it," I breathed. "That's our school."

FREEDOM SCHOOL

New chairs and desks! A small library with books!
"I'm bringing my pole tomorrow," Tom cried.
"We can catch fish for lunch!"

"Welcome to freedom school," Reverend John told us,
when we'd settled on the benches.
"But, sir, what about the law?" Mary asked.
"James knows about the law," said Reverend John. "Can you tell them?"

I stood as tall as I could.
"The law says we can't be taught in the State of Missouri.
But we're in the middle of the Mississippi River now.

The river doesn't belong to just one state
—it belongs to the whole country.

The law against learning can't reach us here."
Reverend John smiled, then he laughed out loud.
And we laughed too.
"Now, let's get to work, children," he said. "The sun's up."
And it was.

BEING BRAVE

I've written it out like Mama asked,
but I don't think I'll ever forget.
For I've made up my mind to go to school
till I'm old enough to row the other
children out,
and teach the little ones to read.

I won't forget,
because now I know that being brave
can sometimes be a small thing,

like lighting a candle, opening a book,
or dipping an oar into still, deep water.

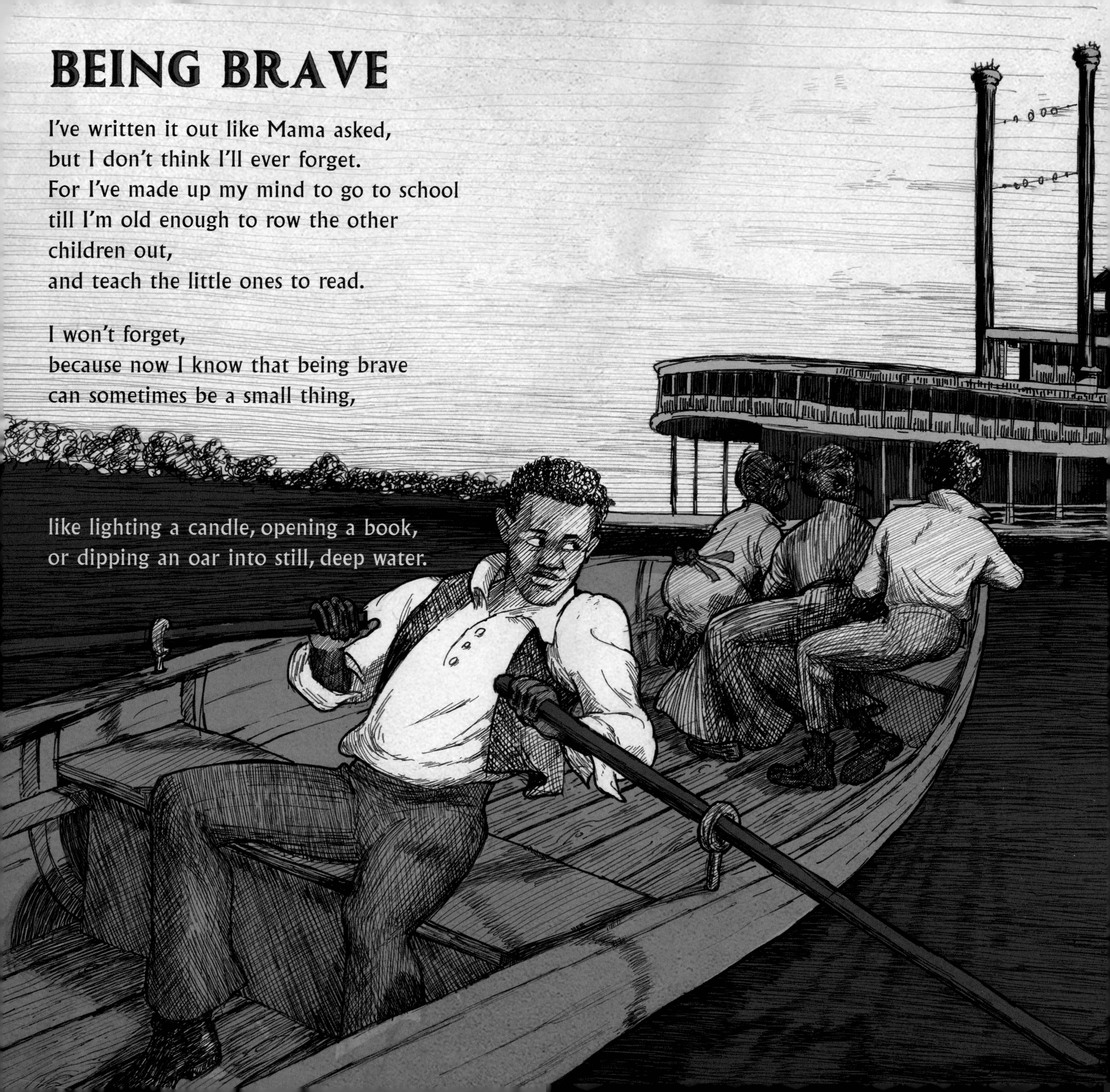

AUTHOR'S NOTE

Steamboat School is a fictional story inspired by the life of Reverend John Berry Meachum (1789–1854). Meachum was a minister, entrepreneur, and educator in St. Louis, Missouri, who fought tirelessly for the rights of African Americans. Born into slavery in 1789 in Virginia, he was brought by his master to North Carolina and Kentucky, where, by 1815, he managed to purchase his own freedom by working in saltpeter mines. He later wrote:

> "Still I was not satisfied, for I had left my old father in Virginia, and he was a slave. It seemed to me, at times, though I was seven hundred miles from him, that I held conversations with him, for he was near my heart. . . .
>
> "In a short time I went to Virginia, and bought my father. . . . My father and myself then earned enough to pay our expenses on the way, and putting our knapsacks on our backs walked seven hundred miles to Hardin county, Kentucky. Here the old man met his wife and all his children, who had been there several years. Oh there was joy!"[1]

1 John Berry Meachum. "An Address to All the Colored Citizens of the United States." Philadelphia. Printed for the author by King and Baird, 1846. *Documenting the American South*, http://docsouth.unc.edu/neh/meachum/meachum.html

Meachum's own wife was still enslaved, so he followed her to St. Louis when her master brought her there. He worked as a carpenter and cooper, and earned money to buy freedom for his wife and children. He also purchased slaves himself. A firm believer in hard work, he then freed them and hired them to work for him until they'd paid him back.

Meachum, whose father was a Baptist preacher, began working with John Mason Peck, a white missionary whose St. Louis congregation included both whites and blacks. Peck also ran a day school for slave children. Meachum was ordained in 1825, and became the leader of a newly formed, separate African American congregation, established as the First African Baptist Church of St. Louis. The community built a new church at Third and Almond Streets in 1827.

Reverend Meachum was passionate about the importance of education, and he continued to run a school in the church's basement. Among the students who attended was James Milton Turner, who later became a consul to Liberia and a prominent St. Louis educator. The boy in this story is named James in Turner's honor, but I could not find any evidence that Turner attended Meachum's new steamboat school, sometimes called the "Floating Freedom School."

Meachum's steamboat school came about in 1847 when a new law against educating blacks forced Meachum to close his "tallow candle school." Meachum found an ingenious solution to the new state law—he moved his school to a steamboat in the Mississippi River, which was considered federal property. Although I have done extensive research and visited the St. Louis Historical Society in St. Louis, I've been unable to find any oral histories or memoirs from anyone who actually attended the school.

Meachum died in 1854. In May 1855 his widow, Mary, was arrested after five runaway slaves who had left from her home were caught crossing the Mississippi River into Illinois. Her home was declared a depot on the Underground Railroad. In 2001, the Mary Meachum Freedom Crossing became the first site in Missouri to be recognized as part of the National Park Service's National Underground Railroad Network to Freedom.

EXPLORE MORE

MISSISSIPPI RIVER

http://www.mvn.usace.army.mil/PAO/history/MISSRNAV/index.asp
History of navigation on the Mississippi River

JOHN BERRY MEACHUM

http://www.umsl.edu/~virtualstl/phase2/1850/people/1850meachum.html
A short piece on John Berry Meachum

MARY MEACHUM AND THE UNDERGROUND RAILROAD

http://www.confluencegreenway.org/locations/mfc.php
All about the Mary Meachum Freedom Crossing

BOOKS FOR YOUNG READERS ON CIVIL RIGHTS AND EDUCATION

Bridges, Ruby. *Through My Eyes*. New York: Scholastic, 1999.

Hopkinson, Deborah. *A Band of Angels: A Story Inspired by the Jubilee Singers*. New York: Atheneum, 1999.

Howard, Elizabeth Fitzgerald. *Virgie Goes to School with Us Boys*. New York: Aladdin, 2005.

Jurmain, Suzanne. *The Forbidden Schoolhouse: The True and Dramatic Story of Prudence Crandall and Her Students*. New York: Houghton Mifflin Books for Children, 2005.

Littlesugar, Amy. *Freedom School, Yes!* New York: Philomel, 2001.

McKissack, Patricia. *Goin' Someplace Special*. New York: Atheneum, 2001.

Paulsen, Gary. *Nightjohn*. New York: Laurel Leaf, 1995.